ABIOSEH NICOL

Two African Tales

THE LEOPARD HUNT
and
THE DEVIL AT YOLAHUN BRIDGE

ILLUSTRATED BY
HASSAN BANGURAH

CAMBRIDGE
AT THE UNIVERSITY PRESS
1965

PUBLISHED BY
THE SYNDICS OF THE CAMBRIDGE UNIVERSITY PRESS

Bentley House, 200 Euston Road, London, N.W. 1
American Branch: 32 East 57th Street, New York, N.Y. 10022
West African Office: P.O. Box 33, Ibadan, Nigeria

ABIOSEH NICOL

1965

Printed in Great Britain at the University Printing House, Cambridge
(Brooke Crutchley, University Printer)

LIBRARY OF CONGRESS CATALOGUE
CARD NUMBER: 65-19166

FOREWORD

THESE stories were written some years ago and have now been modified for my young friends to give them an impression of what happened when we were colonial countries under the rule of Europeans. They owe something to European writers like E. M. Forster, Joyce Cary, Graham Greene and Evelyn Waugh, all of whom I admire and who, themselves, wrote about similar situations. However, being both black and African, I was then on the other side of the fence and perhaps saw things somewhat differently.

Since our national independence, much has changed for the better. White and black people can now more easily be friends and equals in many parts of Africa.

But even in the colonial past, it was sometimes possible for them to respect each other.

I hope these two stories show that.   A.N.

LONDON, 1965.

To my family
with love

The Leopard Hunt

HIS gun was levelled at a spot ten yards from him, and in a direct line along the path of the beast as it made for him. He heard the pebbles rolling and crunching under its great paws as the leopard quickened its pace. He heard the quietness surging around as the rest of the crowd stood in their positions

afraid to shoot for fear they would hit him. He felt a small pebble underneath his right foot as he steadied his balance; and then there was a tiny salty burning drop of sweat trembling on his right eyelash stinging his eye slightly. 'A steady hand, and a true heart; you must keep your side up....' Lord, I forgot the ointment in my pocket, he thought. An instant before the yellow and brown patch flashed before his sight, he pulled the trigger deliberately and the angry roar of the bullet re-echoed from among the rocks. He slipped. There were shouts from around, of terror, dismay and of hoplessness. As he tried to straighten up, he saw the curved arc of the leopard's spring concluding itself on him. And in that second they looked straight into each other's eyes. And then he did not feel so much afraid any longer. The long past years and the lost hopes, fused into a trembling crystal of pain and some sweetness. So this was it.

*   *   *

Mallam Abu Bakar slowly chewed some kola and nodded reflectively. 'In times gone past', he said to those sitting and standing around, 'I would have gone out myself and shot this leopard with my own hands.'

He fingered a dangerous looking rusty Dane gun. There was a murmur of admiration from his courtiers. He was an old minor chieftain in a Northern province who ruled his five or so square miles according to his whim.

'In my youth and prime, I could have killed this beast with my own hands. Ah, but now the strength is gone from them.'

'You have gained in wisdom what you have lost in strength', one of his counsellors comforted.

'Allah be praised', Mallam said modestly. 'There was a time', he continued, 'before the British came, when I rode and fought in my father's army. You could ride for a whole day without pausing and yet not come to the boundaries of my father's kingdom', he said in careless hyperbole. 'You could stand on a hill and look all round without seeing the ground for the number of my father's men.'

'What you have lost in numbers you have gained in respect and love. We know for certain that even now your name makes men tremble', another courtier said.

The few subjects who were left in the three or four villages over which the Mallam ruled knew the old man's fondness for fantasy and exaggeration, and they all humoured him. He was an old man of about eighty, still very active, who spent half the day holding forth and listening to innumerable disputes, and the other half sleeping. His main preoccupation was to find ways of slighting the neighbouring and more powerful provincial chief since he believed that, but for an accident of history and birth—not altogether fortuitous, he would add, with a meaningful expression when addressing his courtiers on this, his favourite topic—he should have been in his place at the head of the province.

He stroked his beard reflectively. 'Tell me more about this leopard', he said to the messenger prostrate in front of him.

'It is an old beast, Highness. It used to kill cattle, but has lately attacked a child, wounding it before being scared off. They say a long time ago this same beast was a pet of white men before escaping into the bush. But now it has come back.'

'Has anyone seen it with their own eyes?' the Mallam asked.

'Some saw him at close quarters, Highness, and one man said that in the under belly of the beast he'd seen something like khaki trousers.'

'What foolishness is this?' the Mallam said sternly. 'I have travelled far and I have heard such stories, but such a thing never has occurred in my father's vast kingdom. We make no

3

medicine of such heathen sort. There is only one God, Allah, and Muhamed is His Prophet.'

'The selfsame man who said he saw this thing of the trousers is known to all to be a half-blind and simple man, Highness', said the messenger humbly.

'Take a horse', the Mallam said, with decision, 'and ride to the white man who is Resident and tell him from me that I and my people want him to come and help us kill the leopard as all

our young men have gone to the town, and anyway, this is not our hunting season. Tell him I have sent directly to him instead of through the provincial chief because the matter is urgent. Lives are lost daily and this is a beast, the cunning of which is great. Ride through the market place and let it be known, so that it comes to the ears of the provincial chief himself, that the great Mallam has sent a messenger to his friend the Resident.' The old man got up triumphantly, dismissed his court and went in to sleep.

★   ★   ★

The Resident was a tall, thin, spare man, in his late forties, grey at the temples, with startling blue eyes. He had two or three large chiefdoms in his province, and a host of minor chieftaincies. He carried out his duties through his District Officers with what he would be happy to hear described as efficiency and British fair play. He befriended the provincial chiefs and played polo with them. He was courteous to the less important chiefs. He allowed himself only official opinions to his fellow Europeans, but moved amongst all, black and white, with easy relaxation. Nothing startling had happened to make him feel that he could go much further in the Administration, and he felt he had been luckier than most. He genuinely enjoyed his work. He was a happy man.

'This thing shouldn't come to me at all, you know, Aitkens', he said, speaking to his District Officer. 'The Mallam knows quite well he ought to report it to his senior chief first, who should then only ask for our help if he thinks it necessary. Mallam Abu Bakar seems to be unaware of the importance of our Native Administration methods.'

'Or I should say he is too much aware of them', said Aitkens. He was a jovial man much the same age as the Resident. 'I should say he is simply trying to pull a fast one over his superior. He delights in annoying him, as he thinks, he ought to be in his position.

'We cannot allow it, you know, we cannot. We must send the messenger back.'

'Righto.'

'Wait', the Resident said suddenly; the thrill of a leopard hunt was too much for him. 'Is this a really serious matter?'

Aitkens himself was partial to the excitement of the chase. 'Well from what one can make out', he said, 'this animal seems to be quite a danger to life and property.'

'It wouldn't do if something happened in the meantime, would it?'

'No, I don't suppose it would.'

'Ah well, I expect we should go. Although, mind you, warn the old rascal that this is a very special case, and in future he must go through the usual drill.

There was a pause. 'Find out some more details', he said, in a different tone of voice.

Aitkens had thought that Burrowes would succumb eventually to trying out the new gun he had brought back from home leave. He'd got all the details worked out.

'From what I can gather, the leopard is hiding in a lair among the rocks in this patch of open country just outside the town.' He produced a map.

'You haven't wasted much time, have you?' Burrowes said, smiling.

'It was last seen the day before yesterday bounding back there after it had been frightened from the bush by people beating drums and tin-cans.'

'It might have moved then.'

'I should doubt it. They kept a pretty close watch all

yesterday and, besides, it had something in its mouth, when it disappeared. It should be getting hungry again now, and will probably come out again soon. Now appears to be the time.'

'Now, let's see', Burrowes said, drawing a piece of paper and pencil towards him. 'Let's make up a shooting party. The two of us, then Reynolds and Watson, our Assistant District Officers. Then there's Skillen of the Police, Jenner and Crabbe, his assistants. Then there's Lewis, the Commercial Agent.'

'Ah, we mustn't forget the Reverend Edward Jennings, our fighting man of God', Aitkens added.

'Yes, Jennings', Burrowes agreed. 'He is a good man with a gun. We need a tenth man', he added, reflectively. For some unknown reason, Burrowes always preferred things in round numbers.

'What about Haworth, the schoolmaster? He's four miles out of town, but we can pick him up on the way.'

'I don't know about him. He is said to be a man who has principles. About such things, of course', he added hastily.

'What about Monsieur Lefevre, then, our gallant ally? He of the French Company?'

'We'd better not ask him', Burrowes replied. 'The thing might become international, if there was an accident, and there might have to be an Exchange of Notes. No, let's try Haworth. Let's be fair to the man.'

And so chits were sent to most of the white population that morning, and there were enthusiastic replies. They stopped work for the day at eleven, and went back to their bungalows to clean their guns.

Mr Banjola, the African clerk in the Resident's office, was sent on a bicycle to Haworth, who was Principal of the Government High School just outside the town. He was ushered into

the Principal's office and asked to sit down. He did so, slightly uncomfortably, and handed the note over. Haworth, as was his custom with all letters borne to him by educated Africans, read it aloud. He believed that the future of the Common-wealth and Empire could only be maintained by complete openness. He made his teachers write their annual confidential reports on themselves.

'Dear Haworth', he read out, 'We are arranging a leopard hunt in the neighbourhood this evening at 5. If you feel like handling a gun, we would appreciate it. I can pick you up on our way there at about 4.30. Yours sincerely, William Burrowes. P.S. This is rather a dangerous animal and has destroyed lives, so it's more an essential piece of work than simply sport. W.B.'

Banjola, although pretending not to, listened with keen interest.

'Tell Mr Burrowes that I'm afraid I can't come. In fact,

I'll write him a note. Just sit down at the typewriter over there and run it off for me. I'll write in the "Dear Burrowes". Just say "I'm sorry I cannot come. As I think you know, I disagree with violence in any form. I'm sure that there must be some more humane method of killing the animal than shooting it. If it is man-eating, it must be that it is because it is old and weak. I can give you some poison which, put on a bait, will destroy the animal painlessly and effectively".'

'Right, thank you, Mr Banjola', he said. After the clerk had gone he sat still for a moment looking out of the window on to the green fronds of the palms lining the drive, and listened to the distant harmony of a singing class somewhere in the building. I hope I haven't offended Burrowes, he thought, but he probably only asked me out of politeness. How hard it is to reconcile oneself sometimes.

★ ★ ★

Banjola turned round quickly to Burrowes who nodded. He slowed down the car gently to a stop. The following cars in the line also ground down their brakes. Banjola, driving the Resident's car with the small Union Jack fluttering on its bonnet, was feeling particularly pleased with himself. On bringing back Haworth's note, Burrowes had asked him outright whether he knew what its contents were, and he had told him that he had typed it for the Headmaster. Burrowes had sat back, thinking. After all, these Africans want self-government, and they ought to begin to learn how to defend their own country and people; they must learn to take responsibility and face danger; we must convert them from a nation of clerks and lawyers to one of action; I shall take the risk and perhaps that's why I will never be a Governor, taking risks unnecessarily and staking my reputation on Africans. He knew it was not the policy of Government to encourage the use of firearms, especially of the Junior Staff. Anyhow.

'Banjola', he called. There was no answer. 'Mr Banjola', he repeated in a louder voice.

'Sir!' The African clerk appeared from the outer office. He stood, hands by his side, pencil wedged behind his ear, quiet, amiable and non-committal. Young, about thirty-three years old although, for official purposes, twenty-six, he had about him an absence of insolence and defiance and a presence of stability and steady doggedness which amused and pleased his British superiors at most times but irritated them when they were feeling ruffled themselves. 'He has the makings of a good chief clerk, but not that of an administrator', they had summed him up in his confidential file.

'Didn't you hear me when I first called?'

'No, sir.'

I am sure he did, but it is a sterile point to press.

'Have you ever used a gun?' Burrowes said aloud.

'Yes, I have, sir.' He wanted to add, because he admired Haworth, 'but I don't believe in violence, sir!' But he did not. The palms of his hands were tingling, however. Instead he said, 'I was a rifle-instructor in the army, sir, and I once belonged to a hunting society, sir.'

'Do you hunt now?'

Banjola looked closely at Burrowes and wondered whether this was a trap. He hunted sometimes, shooting guinea-fowl, hares and small antelopes, but he had not bothered to apply for a gun licence as he did not think it would be granted and, in any case, the fee was too high.

'No, I don't hunt now, sir; I haven't a licence', he added, self-righteously.

'I want you to join us in this leopard hunt.'

'I haven't a gun, sir', Banjola said, pushing down the feeling of exaltation and excitement.

'I shall lend you one. By the way, can you manage a borrowed gun?'

'I will try, sir. I have no licence, sir', he repeated, putting up one last obstacle, his Civil Service training reasserting itself.

'Pass over the Licensing Book for firearms.' Banjola passed it over. Burrowes wrote out a licence to use a gun for a day instead of the usual year, gravely stamped it and signed it. He tore it off and handed it to Banjola. The latter read it, folded it and put it in his pocket. 'What time do you want me, sir?'

'You can go home now, but come to my house at four to see the gun. You will have to drive, as we need all available space.'

'It's all right, sir', Banjola replied, and left.

'Do you think it's wise to ask him?' Aitkens the District Officer had just come in and nodded in the direction of the departing African.

'Yes, I think so. His Army record says he was an efficient marksman', he answered, wilfully refusing to understand the other's question.

'Ah, yes, of course, Resident', Aitkens said, hastily, understanding the other's desire to misunderstand him.

Banjola went home and told his wife, with assumed nonchalance, 'I am going out shooting with those Europeans.'

'What Europeans?'

'Burrowes, Aitkens and the usual crowd. We are going to shoot a leopard.'

'Which leopard?'

'The one troubling people in that town ten miles away.'

'They say it isn't a real leopard at all, but a sorcerer.'

'That's nonsense; it's just an old leopard.'

'But you haven't got a licence?' she asked hopefully.

'The Resident made me out one with his own hands.'

'Oh, Banjola, I am sure no good can come of this. They probably are going to push you in front of this wild beast whilst they all stay behind. Why else should they go to all this trouble to get you to come and hunt with them?' She began to cry, and to wring her hands.

'They are better than that, they have principles', he said, vaguely patting her shoulders. 'They meant to do me honour. It's like asking me to tea.'

'All right, dear, all right.' She wiped her eyes and blew her nose. 'When do they want you?'

'At four.'

She laid out a well pressed khaki shirt and shorts and cleaned his boots well, so that all and sundry would know that he had a good and interested wife. She then slipped away.

At ten to four she reappeared and shyly said to him, 'Husband, would you do me a favour?'

'Why, don't you want me to go?' he asked.

'Oh, yes, you can shoot as well as any of them, if not better.' She paused.

'Yes?'

'I have got a little ointment here which I bought from a wise old man.'

'You mean a witch-doctor', he said grimly.

'Oh, don't be difficult. It is an ointment all hunters used before you or I were born. It clears your sight and ensures that you do not miss. You simply smear it on your forehead and rub it into your palms. Please, dear', she added, seeing his face hardening.

'But you and I were born and brought up Christians. Don't you believe any longer?'

'I do, dear, but this is different. Even you yourself say white men keep a dried rabbit's foot in their pockets for luck. Please do this for my sake. I shall be so disappointed and would never forgive myself if you went without it and something happened to you. Use it just to please your poor, uneducated wife who loves you.' She produced a small packet of ointment which he took unwillingly. 'I'll rub it on later on', he said; 'just before the hunt.' He put it in his pocket, fully intending to throw it away as soon as he was out of sight. She waved to him from the doorway.

'Good-bye, Sir, and don't forget', she said.

He strode in the direction of the Resident's house and, soon afterwards, after trying Burrowes' old gun for feel, he took the wheel of the car and drove off with Aitkens and Burrowes in the back of the car, the long line of cars belonging to the other Europeans streaming behind. They took the road to Kotonkoro at the foot of the hills.

*　　*　　*

They reached the spot where the guides were waiting for them. It was a rocky terrain with one or two caves in the centre. A hundred yards or so distant it gave way to bush, and high grass. The guides pointed out the hollow into which the leopard had last been seen disappearing. There was only one entrance—there was no other exit. Burrowes held a council of war.

'The thing's not so difficult, after all', he said. 'All we have to do is to make a circle around, put a second line of guns in front of the bush, should it get through the circle. We'll then try to get him out and shoot him as he makes for the open. Only one man shoots at a time, if the beast comes within his arc;

if it gets through, the second line has him. And don't go taking pot shots at each other!'

Aitkens did not think this was the best plan, but did not say so.

'Well, how do we get him out?' someone asked.

'We'll starve him to submission', someone said, with a titter, 'and he might even come out with the white flag.'

Burrowes pretended not to hear.

'We can make a noise', someone suggested.

'Yes', Burrowes turned to him enquiringly, 'that's a good suggestion.'

'Or we can shoot straight into the hole', someone else added.

'I've an idea', another said. 'We can prod him out. The cave can't be very deep and there are rain holes at the top. A spear tied to a long stick would be just the thing.'

'Yes, that sounds feasible.'

'Who's going to prod him out?' Aitkens asked. 'I mean, we need every gun', he added hastily.

'I'll do it', Jennings offered.

'We'll let one of the guides do it', Burrowes decided. 'The top of the cave is quite high and they can use their own spears best.'

They all covered the entrance of the cave with their guns whilst one of the guides climbed gingerly to the top. Then Burrowes started arranging them.

'You stand here, Jennings', pointing to a position. He arranged them carefully so that none faced each other. He put Watson, the youngest, between Jennings and Banjola, and arranged them at the rear of the cave, where he thought the leopard was least likely to go. After arranging the others, he strolled to his own position in a straight line in front of the entrance to the cave and aimed .... Then he put his gun

14

down, checked the safety catch, cupped his hand and shouted to the guide.

'Pu-u-u-sh!!!'

          ★   ★   ★

The European doctor accelerated furiously up to breakneck speed for a few seconds; then slowed down, stopped and reversed slowly. Yes, he had got it, he discovered triumphantly. He had been trying to run down a sanake which was crossing the road in front of his car. He was on the point of getting out to examine the crushed snake more closely when he remembered it might have a mate so he decided to stay in the car and look at it from there. It was a big one, about six feet long and black. A poisonous one, a mamba, its middle still rippling slowly in the violence of its recent death. The ants would soon be on to it in their orderly black inexorable columns picking its flesh, and, in a matter of a day or two, only its sinuous bleached skeleton would be left across the road to be washed away sometime by the torrential rain. Doc Bradshaw shuddered slightly and started off again, slowly. He knew this road well. He glanced to the left to watch the rocks, great and small, casting their jagged shadows behind them and climbing steeply to the mighty plateau, and then looked to the right at the short wild glory of the twilight. He had always wished he could paint. It seemed such a pity that someone could not entrap this symphony of light and beauty for ever. There was in it a soft mellifluous pink at the edges, deepening to a clamorous red around the middle where the coppery half disc of the sun waited hesitantly in this western sky. Farther away there were strands of delicate green nestling within a hollow resounding yellowish-blue. A few white clouds above caught some of the colours and re-echoed them down in a warm ethereal note. And then the darkness softly rushed in and the sky was an inverted bowl of topaz with wisps of reminiscent pink and greyish white lingering by, like a half-remembered melody. He loved the country. A small man, with a leather-tanned face and completely grey hair, he had long passed the age of retirement from the Medical Missionary Service, but he had refused to return home. With no family ties at all, he had decided to die here, where he had known happiness, and the simple friendship of the peasants. Now he was on his way to one of his branch dispensaries twenty miles away from his hospital. He would sleep there in the small wooden hut, hold a religious service in the morning, run a clinic of the more difficult cases which his African assistant had reserved for him, and then drive back. He did this once a fortnight.

'Coo-eee.' He stopped when he heard the call and waited. A horseman on a white charger drew up and told him that there had been a big accident, a big accident indeed, and the Resident, himself, in his own very person, had sent him, the messenger, for doctor. A white man was involved, he added impressively.

'What was it?' Doc Bradshaw asked, 'Car accident, snake-bite, sui—' he stopped himself, 'shooting accident?'

It was a leopard, the messenger told him, a leopard which had torn several men to pieces.

'Any dead?'

'They are pouring with blood, absolutely pouring.'

Probably one man mauled, the doctor thought. Messengers for doctors usually laid it on, for effect, and to make sure he would turn back.

'What about the leopard?'

'It paid with its life', was the dramatic reply.

'All right. I'll come.'

The horseman salaamed, turned round and galloped off down the road into the darkness.

Bradshaw turned and drove quickly down the road, his headlights two pencil beams in the darkness. The tropical insects rushed in to his windscreen in tiny streaks like minute tracer bullets. At last he reached the town, with hundreds of oil-lamps flickering along the roadside by the market stalls. He drove straight to the hospital, skipped out and bounded up the stone steps. He found Burrowes pacing up and down the corridor, an alert, anxious figure.

'Glad you could come, Bradshaw. There has been an accident. Aitkens is slightly hurt, and Banjola, my clerk, has been badly mauled by a leopard.'

'Whom would you like me to see first?'

'I think Banjola; he is more seriously hurt. He is somewhere in there with your nursing sister and orderlies.' Bradshaw disappeared through the door and Burrowes went downstairs to the waiting room.

*　　*　　*

Two days later Banjola was well enough to see visitors. His wife, had been allowed to see him the first night, to dispel rumours that he was dead. Burrowes called to see him the second day, by his bedside, chatted for a few minutes and reassured him that his family would be looked after well during his illness. Banjola had been placed in one of the two private wards reserved for Europeans who periodically went down with malaria or dysentery. He was in the D room which was quieter and had a bathroom attached. There was a mass of flowers in his room from the other members of the hunting party. He woke up after some hours to find himself almost completely bandaged from head to foot with a searing pain across his chest. He tossed about wearily for a bit and was given morphia again. After two days he was more conscious of his surroundings, although weak. His wife usually sat quietly with him for half an hour a day, in the evenings, telling him occasionally of what was happening in the town, of the songs they had made in his praise and the visits she had received from the local press agents of the big newspapers in the south. On the third day she asked him whether he was strong enough to see a visitor for a few minutes.

'Who is it?' he asked.

'Oh, someone I know', she said avoiding his eyes. She went out and brought him in. He was an old African with an almost completely white beard, a turban round his head. His face was lined and impressive, his teeth stained red with chewing kola nuts, his nose slightly aquiline, his eyes fixed and piercing. She introduced Banjola to him. 'This is my husband, old father, whose life you have helped us to save.'

'I'm glad, my daughter', he said, standing beside the bed. Banjola looked from him to her and back again. He didn't remember him. He had wondered whether this was the guide. Ayo saw the look of interrogation on his face and said: 'This is the old man who sold me the ointment.'

'Which ointment?'

'The one which you used and which helped you with the hunting', she said.

'The one which confused the leopard and killed it', the old man corrected.

'I didn't use the ointment', Banjola said, looking at his wife. She looked away out of the window, at a pink cloud in the greying sky. 'I threw it away', he said angrily.

'They found it in your pocket', she said, still not looking at

18

him. 'The hospital attendants removed it and gave it to me so that the white men would not see it.'

'I didn't use it', he said, 'I'd forgotten it was there. I meant to throw it away.'

'It was a warm afternoon', the old man said, sternly, 'and some of it melted and stained your trouser pocket. A little of it must have touched the skin of your leg. That was what saved your life. If you had rubbed it properly, all this'—he swept his hand round the hospital room—'wouldn't have happened.'

'Oh, take him away', Banjola said, wearily, and he turned

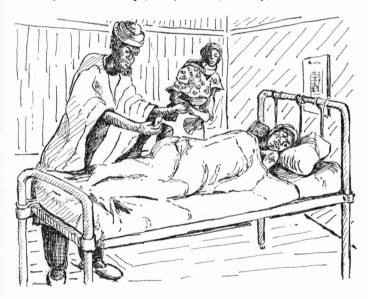

his head from them to the other side. He turned round again suddenly and looked the old man straight in the eye.

'And you can take your rubbish juju away too', he said.

'Oh, Banjola', his wife said, startled by his disrespect for age and his lack of fear.

'I will go away', the old man said in his resonant voice. And now he and the sick man were looking steadily at each other. 'But tell me this before I go, you foolish man', he said scornfully, 'when that leopard was rushing for you and all your friends the white men with their magic and their guns couldn't do anything, did you not think of my medicine? Did you not remember it?' he said, thrusting his head forward.

Banjola half lifted his head from the pillow. It was true. He had remembered it in his pocket. 'Go away', he said, weakly, angrily groping for the bell.

'It's all right, Sir, it's all right, Sir, we'll go', his wife said to him, leading the old man away. The old man walked off triumphantly because he thought he'd seen doubt in Banjola's eyes and felt he had not altogether lost.

'It is a good thing you bought the medicine for him', he said outside, with an air of tolerance and sagacity, to her. 'It would have been hard for you to find such another husband if he had been killed. He is a man with spirit who is very sick in body now and a little sick in mind. You were wise to buy my ointment.'

She thanked him and returned to the room to make peace.

'What do you mean by bringing him in here?' said Banjola, weak with anger. She sank into the chair beside him, and lowered her head in her hands.

'Why do you shame me before our people like this, my husband? Couldn't you have said a simple 'Thank you'? After all, he was just trying to help us. What has come over you of late?' Her voice was low, but vibrant with anger and sorrow. 'You never seem satisfied with anything now. You never used to be like this when you first married me. You used to say that we must keep something of our African past and be proud of it. But now, when I wear African clothes you point to other women who wear modern frocks; when I wear a frock you say I look much nicer in African dress. Are you sorry you married me ? Are you dissatisfied with me ?'

She took a deep breath and stared stonily at the ground. She was unused to talking for so long, but was moved by a mounting unhappiness. Banjola moved his left arm slowly and painfully put it on her lap.

'No', he said, slowly and thoughtfully, 'perhaps it's myself I'm not satisfied with. They say I lack leadership', he said irrelevantly.

'What's that got to do with it ?' she asked, mollified by his gesture.

'They say I can't lead men, that we all can't lead men, but they haven't tried us out. They haven't tried us out', he continued half-dreamily. 'No', he shook himself, 'it has nothing to do with it', he said, 'I'm sorry I was rude to the old man. Thank him for me, but thank you more, for thinking about my safety. I have such a good wife.'

The nurse entered the room and took in the situation at a glance, and said 'I'll come again to make the bed.'

'No, I'm going now. Visiting hours are over', said Banjolas' wife, relaxing into her usual meek and law-abiding self.

*   *   *

Banjola spent a restless night after the visit of the old man. He woke up once or twice, with a start, to feel the reassuring tenseness of his bandages. He dreamt that the leopard jumped at him and, halfway through its leap, changed to the old magician, who knocked him down and started rubbing him all over with a pungent ointment which burnt through his skin like fire. He screamed with pain, and beat feebly against the air, waking up. The night nurse came in and gave him an injection. After that, he slept deeply till morning. It was just over a week since the accident. The doctor was surprised and pleased that the wounds had not festered.

'I have good blood', Banjola told him, shyly. His wife and son visited him that morning and Banjola told them the good news that he was to get up that afternoon for the first time as the doctor thought that he had been lying still too long. Banjola played with his son a little and asked him whether he would like to be a doctor and make sick people well. 'No', the boy said, stoutly, he would like to drive a big lorry and brake and change gear and go Br-r-r-r boop, boop, boop and smoke would come out of his lorry's tail and people would run away from the road when they saw him coming, driving his lorry. His father smiled and promised him a toy lorry for Christmas.

Visiting hours were soon over. The male nurse then came round. He smiled amiably. He was pleasant to Banjola because he was a hero and because his wife had taken the precaution of tipping him five shillings to make sure he looked after Banjola well.

'Doctor is coming, and we are going to try to make you take small small walk', he said.

Soon the doctor arrived and they slowly propped Banjola up. He felt very weak. 'Now feet on the ground', Doc Bradshaw said. 'We shall just take two or three steps today. Rest your weight on both of us.'

They gently helped him to an upright position. He took one step forward, haltingly. Then, very slowly, another.

'Are you all right?' Doc Bradshaw asked him. He nodded. He was on the edge of a sucking whirlpool of fear.

'I think that will be enough for today', Doc said. 'We shall put you back to bed.'

Suddenly a great murmuring filled Banjola's ears. He felt

22

an extraordinary urgency to use the bed pan and he said faintly, 'The pot, the pot.' A film of reddish darkness rose before his eyes and a tremendous suffocation oppressed him. He pushed both men away and tore at his neck with superhuman desperation. It was as if he were being swirled into a hopeless vacuum. Then he slumped forward.

Doc Bradshaw sprang forward and crouched over Banjola on the floor and started applying artificial respiration, steadily and swiftly. 'Adrenaline! The emergency tray!' he shouted to the nurse. The latter dashed off and soon returned, followed by half the hospital staff.

'Oxygen', Doc said.

'We ran out last week, Sir, I forgot to tell you', the nurse said, wringing his hands.

'Take over then', and the doctor got up carefully whilst the male nurse immediately took over the rhythmic movements of artificial respiration.

Doc Bradshaw checked the ampoule and gave the injection. Then he put his stethoscope to Banjola's chest and listened carefully. He got up. 'Stop', he said to the nurse. 'Go away back to your work', he said, irritably, to the others standing round. They started moving off. The male nurse wept. 'I am sorry about the oxygen, Sir.'

'Indent for it at once', Doc Bradshaw said firmly. 'It would not have helped here, anyway', he added, kindly. 'Help me lift the body on to the bed and then go and call Mr Burrowes, the Resident.'

Burrowes was in the middle of a round of golf when the news reached him. He left immediately, accompanied by Aitkens. Doc Bradshaw took them to his office and talked about it.

'I think a large blood clot must have moved into his lungs—

a pulmonary embolus. He did not stand a chance when that happened.'

'What a disaster!' Burrowes said, puckering his lips thoughtfully. He was more upset than he showed.

'Would you like me to do a post-mortem?' Bradshaw asked. 'You know how strenuous objections are to that out here', he added.

'I think you should', Burrowes replied, 'and there will have to be an inquest. I cannot be the coroner, of course, as I shall have to give evidence. Neither can you, Aitkens, as you have to also. We shall have to get someone up from the capital.'

Burrowes and Aitkens drove back from the hospital, and Aitkens dropped off at the European Club. Burrowes said he had a headache and drove home. The other Europeans were gathered in the smoking room waiting for news. Aitkens told them. They were silent, all thinking the same thing but not saying it. At last a senior merchant spoke up. 'He should not have taken the African on the shoot. There were bound to be difficulties in any case.' 'He had a good motive', Aitkens said. He clapped his hands vigorously and the steward came running in. He changed the subject and ordered drinks.

⋆　　⋆　　⋆

The inquest took place in a small schoolroom a week later. Most of the British population were there, and some of the educated Africans who were not in Government service. Dr Jolson, the coroner, had come up from the capital. To save any future doubt of impartiality, he had stayed at the Club and had his meals there instead of with Burrowes or with any of the other Europeans. This was necessary, as the nationalist papers in the big cities had started featuring the affair.

24

According to them, Banjola had been forced to take part in a leopard hunt, had been put in a vulnerable and dangerous position, badly armed, whilst the British had stayed at a safe distance; he had naturally been mauled to death.

A lawyer had been briefed by a nationalist political party to come up and attend the inquest in the interests of Banjola's family.

Newi, the lawyer, sat in impregnable silence, taking notes, during the opening portion of the inquest. He had only smiled once, and that was when Jolson had asked Mrs Banjola whether she wished to be represented by Newi. 'Yes', she had said. She had been overwrought since Banjola's death. In her distress and confusion she felt obscurely that Banjola was to blame for not having used the ointment. The old magician had turned up soon after the funeral to explain that what little of the ointment had touched Banjola's leg through his trouser pocket must have been neutralised by Banjola's general unwillingness.

Various groups of people had called to see her, and her brother, too, had arrived. He told her that the case was going to be fought and there would be money in it for her. He brought some of the newspapers up for her and read them to her. She had mildly protested, on listening, and said that Banjola himself had wanted to go on the hunt and was not forced. Her brother had corrected her, angrily. 'Newspapers never lie', he had said; 'what they say here, in this paper, must be the truth', he had added, as an afterthought. 'And, indeed, my dear sister, you must speak no evil of the dead; your husband was a good man.' So she had listened patiently and, afterwards, kept in her trunk the newspapers and all the others following, which had reported the incident.

Burrowes had visited Mrs Banjola soon after her husband's

death, but her relations had hurriedly pushed her and her son into a back room and her brother had told him sullenly that she was out. Burrowes had then, for the first time, recognised that it was not only his fellow-British who were against him over the hunting accident.

Newi had arrived the day before the inquest and he had been welcomed at a small reception at the house of Mr Obeong, the senior African. He had made a short speech telling them that the political party existed to fight for their freedom. Then he had called for membership enrolment. There had been a brisk response, but not all paid their entrance fees. They promised to send it on later. Newi was used to this state of affairs. Later that evening he had briefed Mrs Banjola about her evidence the next day.

And now she sat, with hands clasped on her lap, listening as the inquest went on. Doc Bradshaw gave evidence and the results of his post-mortem. Death was due to pulmonary embolism. A long clot of blood had shifted from a large vein and lodged in one of the main blood vessels of one of the deceased's lungs. Deceased had previously been given full treatment and bed rest for his injuries. There had been every hope of recovery, but this unforeseen and rare complication had caused death. Newi questioned a few details of treatment but he did not press because he knew Bradshaw was a missionary, well liked by most of the Africans, and one could never tell when one would next need a doctor oneself. However, there was a lively exchange about whether Banjola's death had been caused directly through the injuries caused by the leopard. Bradshaw said that the embolism had no individual connection with the injuries but could have occurred if Banjola had been in bed with any other injury. 'Can you name me anything which would have kept a fit man in bed for eight days?'

26

'Anything; a twisted ankle', Bradshaw hazarded.

'Had the deceased twisted his ankle in this case?' Newi asked, with a great show of cunning.

'Of course not, that was only an example', Bradshaw said.

'Ah!' Newi exclaimed.

('My God, Newi is brilliant', an African muttered into the ears of another. 'Yes, he confuses them', the other replied. 'Silence!' Dr Jolson cried.)

The inquest continued. A few witnesses of the hunting accident and Banjola's collapse at the hospital came forward and gave their evidence. Jolson told Newi several times that his questions were irrelevant. Gradually the complete story unfolded. It had been like this. The leopard, after being prodded several times, leapt out, an enraged yellow blur. Burrowes downed it with one echoing shot. They all relaxed and some started moving forward. Burrowes shouted to them to stop. The leopard sprang off at a tangent and headed in Aitkens' direction. Aitkens lifted gun to shoulder, slipped and fell. Banjola, who had not moved at all, had the flank of the best towards him. He fired. He missed but had distracted the animal towards him. The maddened beast turned to him. The recoil of the unaccustomed gun made Banjola stagger back, but he regained an insecure foothold on the loose rocks. The leopard charged him. He was in the line of fire and no one was on the other side to help. Banjola waited for a second or two to make sure he would not miss, then fired again. The leopard knocked him down and, with a great shudder, died on him. When they reached him, Banjola was unconscious. He had lacerated wounds on his thighs and shoulders where he had been clawed.

Doc Bradshaw thought that he had lost consciousness through shock and hitting his head against a rock when he was knocked down. His wounds had been severe but not actually crippling.

Newi questioned Burrowes with ferocity. 'Was it not well known that when a leopard left a dark hole it turned round and charged what was behind it?' Burrowes said this was very new to him; where did Mr Newi get his information? 'Everybody who has taken the trouble to read Hargenstein's Textbook on Wild Game knew this elementary fact,' Newi replied. 'And, therefore', he continued, 'the deceased had been put in the most dangerous position.' Jolson asked sharply where a copy of the authority quoted could be found. 'In London', Newi answered. 'If it cannot be produced, then it is inadmissible', Jolson said.

Newi began again, elaborately; he was not aware, he said, that the late Mr Banjola could afford such an expensive rifle as that which he had used. Burrowes, who had kept his temper throughout, began to show signs of strain.

'I loaned him the gun', he said shortly.

'You have two, then, Sir?' Newi asked.

'Yes. I had two. I loaned him the older one because I knew that better; I did not want him to use the new one which had not been tried out.'

This cut the ground from under Newi's feet. He could no longer suggest that Banjola had been given an old and useless gun.

'Had Mr Banjola a licence?' he continued.

'Yes', Burrowes answered. He knew that Newi knew perfectly well that Banjola had one, and the circumstances in which it had been given.

'It is curious that it bears the date the hunt took place. Perhaps that was the day everyone took out licences?' Newi asked heavily.

Burrowes replied that he had asked Banjola whether he would like to join the hunt and, on the latter agreeing, had lent him his gun; he had then issued him with a licence to regularise the position. At the shoot, despite Mr Newi's zoological authorities, he had put Banjola in the least dangerous position for no other reason than because he was the most junior in rank amongst those present. He would like to testify to Banjola's bravery and courage, apparent and greatly appreciated by all present. Banjola had clearly saved one life and possibly many more. Burrowes stopped. Aitkens nodded vigorously. Dr Jolson took notes.

Suddenly something snapped inside Newi. He had carefully prepared his questions about the various irregularities and had determined to worry and humiliate a Senior Administrative Officer whom he regarded as a natural enemy. It was a wonderful opportunity. Now Burrowes had calmly stated everything in a matter of fact fashion.

'Banjola was sacrificed and killed by you all', Newi shouted towards where the few Europeans sat. 'He was forced and dragooned to accompany you. It is on record that he protested. The office messenger heard him. But a licence was forced on him. He was given an old and useless gun which could not kill a mouse and he was practically thrown into the arms of the leopard. There are his widow and orphaned son. Who will feed them?' he cried, 'Who?'

Newi sat down. There was commotion among the Africans at the back.

The coroner rapped his desk hard. After a while there was silence. He cleared his throat. He tried to lessen the tension with a joke.

'It must be a very large mouse that a heavy calibre gun could not kill.' No one smiled. 'Anyhow, I think, Mr Newi, that

a man belonging to an honourable profession such as yours
would be bound to admit that the suggestions which you have
just made are neither factual nor chivalrous.'

Newi continued sitting in his chair. He leaned back and
closed his eyes. His high forehead and shining baldness glist-
ened with perspiration. Small rivulets of sweat ran down his
face, dropping down on to his London School of Economics
blazer. He knew he should apologise and he knew he would
not do so. He knew that Burrowes was a kind administrator
and better than most, and had asked Banjola along because he
had more faith in Africans than the other Europeans had. He
knew all this because Obeong had told him and he himself was
quite aware of it from the evidence and the situation. He felt
tired and he kept his eyes closed and refused to withdraw.
Why all this strife, he thought. Why all this diffuse hatred
against the British which he whipped up, up and down the
country. He had once liked them. Why this secret envy which
drove him to quote false authorities? What was it he envied,
anyway? Their reputed physical and moral courage? Their
proud straight backs? Their easy air of confidence and of authority, or was it of arrogance? Or was it that they stood between
him and power? Was it as simple as that? Was this the naked
foundation of his idealism and patriotism; that they had the
power which he craved? He had never felt before this doubt
and fear and confusion. He thought 'I must be getting old'.
He decided then that he would apologise and fight clean. But
he sat on. He was afraid if he moved or opened his eyes, he
would sob, so painful was the hardness within him.

The court waited.

Jolson and the other Europeans, looking at Newi's heavy
square mahogany face with its pursed thick lips and clenched
jaw, thought what an obstinate and nasty piece of work the

fellow was. Jolson said, then, 'Since counsel appearing for the relations of the deceased has not had the courtesy to apologise, I must now ask him whether he has any more witnesses he would wish called or anything further to say.'

Newi, still unable to trust himself to speak, shook his head. He had not even bothered to call Mrs Banjola to say how unwilling Banjola had been to join the hunt.

The inquest was adjourned for an hour, after which Jolson announced Death by Misadventure, praising the deceased for gallantry and adding that proper compensation would be paid, as he felt the death of Mr Banjola was directly due to his performing his duty.

The African crowds cheered Newi as they felt he had somehow won the case, witness the fact of the compensation.

He went back to the capital the next day.

Stones were thrown at passing European motorists in the next few days, but the affair was soon forgotten and all was peaceful again. Burrowes went on leave soon after and was transferred to the Far East.

*　　*　　*

'The irony of the whole thing was that, of them all at the inquest, white and black, I think *I* knew Banjola best and liked him most. He had worked for me for five years and I knew he had something in him; he was good material. After his death I had to look through the drawers of his office desk. They were full of correspondence courses on Electrical Engineering, Muscle Building, Effective Personality and Leadership, that the poor chap used to subscribe to and read through office hours! His wife was a quiet, nice looking girl. I wonder what happened to her? But you would not know. All this was a long time ago. Twenty-five or thirty years and, in any case,

31

you come from another part of Africa. Burrowes, ageing with a slight stoop, poured me out another cup of tea. I was one of a group of Commonwealth Local Government Officers who had been sent to a market town in Buckinghamshire to study the intricate workings of an English municipality. Burrowes had heard that there was an African in the town and had made inquiries and asked me to tea. His name struck some vague chord in my memory and I had accepted. He was slightly disappointed that I was not from where he had served. I had not bothered to tell him that my mother was a widow from his former province and had married again and we had all gone off to settle in another part of Africa. Conversation was rather halting at first, and we talked about my work and the British Social Services. I had then remarked what a fine leopard skin with stuffed head he had hanging on the wall. Then he had told me this story. It had taken a long time, and by the time he had finished, the autumn evening was dark.

'I often wondered too, what happened to Newi; he seemed a very embittered man', Burrowes said, again reminiscing.

I told him that Newi was now one of Her Majesty's most distinguished judges. He was surprised. 'How do you know?' he asked. 'You are a long way from Nigeria.' 'Oh, you see these things in the papers', I said, 'they all carry 'interterritorial news.' He was satisfied. 'Tell me', he said with sudden curiosity 'has he been knighted?' 'Yes', I replied, 'he was made a Knight Bachelor in the last New Year's Honours List, 'as Commonwealth judges sometimes are'.

Burrowes put back his head and shook with laughter, 'To think that Newi and I would both end up on the same side of the fence.'

I looked at him questioningly.

'Yes', he continued, 'for a long time after my transfer from Nigeria, I thought, in fact, was fairly certain, that I was in disgrace; and so did my friends. But the war came, and times changed. Our whole outlook altered. Those of us in the Colonial Service who were prepared to take risks and had faith, found ourselves being rapidly promoted. The whole incident had taught me a great deal. I knew then that if any progress was to be made, we had to work not only for and with the Banjolas but with the Newis. We had understood the former and quite often underestimated them; we had little time or use for the latter. I learnt my lesson well.' He smiled. 'I ended up with a knighthood as Governor of one of the West Indian Islands', he ended with pride.

I made ready to leave. 'You must have a parting glass of sherry', he insisted, 'and then come and see me often again.' I accepted, and agreed. He went out of the room to fetch glasses.

I walked over to the wall where the leopard hung. I thought why do we carry unnecessary bundles of bitterness inside us through the years thinking they warm us, whilst all they do is to freeze our hearts? So I had kept mine all through childhood and adolescence, reading and re-reading the newspaper cuttings which my mother had kept at the bottom of her trunk.

There hung the leopard, its tail curled, a look of proud silly pessimism on its face; its brownish black spots smaller over its face and paws than over the rest of its body; its whiskers stiff; its fangs bared; and its protruding tongue was dry, pinkish-red, glazed, immobile. I stroked its skin gently, with a new lightness within me, and I knew then why my dead father had not been afraid when it had leapt and crushed him down, far, far away, on that rocky hillside in Africa, so long ago.

The Devil at Yolahun Bridge

SANDERSON stirred restlessly in his sleep, and suddenly woke up, as a distant peal of thunder slowly approached overhead. He got up, whisked his mosquito net aside, and groped for his electric torch. He lit it and played its beam into all corners of the room. He walked to the door, pressed his nose against the glass pane and watched the Kissi hills reveal themselves for several seconds in their majestic range before being enveloped again in tropical darkness. He sat down on a wooden easy chair and waited.

He had always been afraid of thunder and lightning and was secretly ashamed of this fear, but he had trained himself to face his fears. He resolved not to wonder whether his bungalow would be struck by lightning. After all it was in the valley, he told himself, and there were many hills and tall trees around. He ought to be quite safe really, and in fact there was a lightning conductor in his roof; but yet he felt uneasy. The wind grew and he felt that the worst of the thunderstorm had passed. He got up, mixed himself a drink and went to bed again. He tried to sleep, but soon gave it up and tried thinking of his next day's work. There were one or two things he remembered he ought to do, and yes, of course, there were the annual report and returns.

Since McPherson had gone away on leave he had kept postponing it. He had received a gentle reminder from the Secretariat a few days ago. He really must finish it soon. He disliked writing reports. He had looked through old copies of past ones and could not believe anybody bothered to read them. He toyed with one or two mad ideas. Suppose he sent, say, the 1923 reports verbatim with a few changes, the name of a sub-chief altered here and the name of a village there; he wondered whether anyone would detect it. Or suppose, say, he sent in some blank sheets with a very impressive folder. But he pushed such thoughts from his mind as too risky. Things which appeared very witty immediately, could easily take on an air of impertinence, incompetence or irresponsibility after travelling for two days or a few hundred miles. He must write the report properly tomorrow; how should he begin? The beginning was always the trouble. He would have to look up copies of reports of past years. He felt he ought to make some new departure. McPherson had always started his by plunging straight into his subject. He would show that a new hand was at the helm. Perhaps he might begin with some short hitherto unknown aspect of Kissiland anthropology which would demonstrate that he took a vital interest in the district and its people.

No, he wouldn't do that. He might be thought scholarly or they might think he was especially interested in the district and leave him there for too long. He would concentrate on the essential things instead—roads, the increase of trade and the shift of the young from the village to the towns. Ah, that was more familiar ground. He fell into a fitful doze.

The next afternoon, he remembered that he had a dictionary and a ready reckoner somewhere which would help him write his report and he started hunting for them. He pulled down a large black tin trunk, dusted the cover and opened it. He did not like to trust his servant Ahmed, or anyone for that matter, with his books. He started searching, removing three or four at a time, till suddenly a large black cockroach dropped from between two and started across the floor. He

picked up the nearest book swiftly and was at the point of
hurling it when Ahmed suddenly opened the door and walked
in. It was a ridiculous position to be found in, with arm up-
lifted. He opened the book quickly and pretended that he
had been reading it, holding it up to catch the light. Ahmed
apologised and moved one or two things silently while
Sanderson noisily turned the pages. Ahmed asked whether
he could do anything to help shift master's books. Master
must ask him to do things for him, that was what he was
there for. Sanderson smiled and thanked him; Ahmed bowed
gravely and departed.

Sanderson looked idly at the book which he had been holding
and discovered that it was an old classical text. He turned to
the fly-leaf and read curiously 'Exlibris Michael St John
Sanderson, Balliol, Michaelmas 1938'. He sat back on his
haunches and idly flicked the pages, and Oxford came back
to him in the dwindling tropical day. He had gone there
young, straight from school. There was a mingled air of
hilarity and inevitability amongst his circle of friends. It had
seemed faintly absurd then to be reading Classics. The idea
of Reading Engineering or Modern Languages or even
Economics had been considered in turn but his uncle had
decided on History or Classics since he couldn't make up
his mind what career he would like to follow.

'Take either of those',—the old man had said, in his study
in the rambling country rectory where Sanderson, orphaned
from an early age, had spent his holidays—'Take either
of those, they will not commit you to anything; and at least
you can change to something later on if you feel like it, without
anyone wanting to know why you changed.'

That was prudent advice, Sanderson thought now in retro-
spect. He had found that wherever he had been since, in the

37

Officers' Training Corps, in the Army itself, and for a short period in business, it had always given him an undeserved aura of being well-educated.

But Oxford, from many points of view, could not be said to have been a complete success. He thought irrelevantly of the High, deserted on an autumn Sunday morning and of cycling up later to North Oxford for tea with his Tutor's family on his first Sunday afternoon. He had spent hours before trying to decide what to wear with the only suit he possessed. He hesitated between his old school tie and his new college tie. He chose the former as being more distinctive. His Tutor might recognise it and this might prove the starting-point of a pleasant and firm friendship between them.

All did not go well, however. When his Tutor's wife called him in a friendly manner, by his first name to give him a cup of tea, his hands trembled so much with nervousness and pleasure that he had dropped the tea in her lap. She leapt up in pain from the settee, steam rising from her dress, and left the room flushed and embarrassed. Sanderson was profusely apologetic. He had wondered gloomily whether he would be sent down from the University for this. When his hostess returned to the room in a new dress, however, she had spoken to him kindly and with understanding.

Sanderson had really never quite got into the habit of systematic work. He attended lectures sporadically and idled away his evenings, attending meetings of various societies and arguing far into the night with friends afterwards. He kept vaguely reassuring himself that this was really what education meant and what Oxford stood for. He would work hard in the vacations to make up for it, he had always said, but when these came he always felt he needed a rest and told himself that anyway, no one, except a few narrow intellectual people who probably had no friends at all, did any work except in the final term. When that arrived, he panicked at the pile of work in front of him and in fact, only a sound sixth-form grounding helped him to be classed at all.

He was secretly surprised that he had passed. He handed the note from his college giving his results across the breakfast table to his uncle.

'From this letter', the old man said, smoothing it, 'your Tutor seems to be glad in a congratulatory way which leads me to suspect that he had feared the worst.' He folded it carefully, and handed it back; continued with his breakfast and reading *The Times*. He never mentioned another word about it again. Sanderson could see that he was deeply disappointed. He vaguely wondered what to do next. He spent a desultory summer. Then the war came and solved it all for him. He joined up.

All through that mad holocaust, there had only been one moment in North Africa, when he felt his former life had not been wasted. They had halted for a moment waiting for supplies. Their speed of advance, coupled with a retreating army in front, and the number of prisoners-of-war they found surrendering, was somewhat embarrassing. He had had an outing one afternoon with Higgins, a REME Lieutenant, to see some ruined Roman fortifications; they had both watched the strange shadows cast by the crumbling bastions across the lovely desert in the setting sun.

'I think this was part of the line of fortifications built by the Emperor Severus in the third century Anno Domini', he had observed to Higgins, not with any intention of displaying erudition, because he was at heart a humble man, but because he was thinking aloud, rebutting the sense of aimlessness and uselessness which sometimes possessed him. They looked at it silently for some time before moving away, each with his own private thoughts. '*Sic transit*' he'd said as they drove away.

Higgins was more prosaic; 'I wish there was some postcards showing the view, which I could have sent home to Mary. She is keen on old ruins, you know. She has an album full of postcards of them. Stonehenge, Fountains Abbey, The British Museum and that sort of thing....'

★   ★   ★

All in all, the dog-eared classical text was to pass through several hands. John Momoh, his junior African clerk picked it up one morning from his desk and took it to the outer office to show the older clerk, Mr Alfred Thomas, an urbane middle-aged African from one of the coastal towns. Momoh himself came from the hinterland and was fond of Mr Thomas. He usually seized every opportunity of entering into conversation with him on matters in which he thought the older man was interested. He knew that Mr Thomas, for all his politeness and deferential behaviour, was faintly hostile to Sanderson, since he felt that McPherson and himself were the only people who knew anything at all about the office and the district. Mr Thomas felt he could quite well have acted in McPherson's absence and he resented Sanderson's acting appointment. He silently resisted by doing only as much as he should, and nothing more. He gave advice only when Sanderson asked for it.

Momoh knew all this, and enjoyed the silent battle which went on. He was an agent provocateur for both sides.

'I did not know Mr Sanderson was Roman', he said bringing the book out and handing it to Mr Thomas. 'I found this Catholic prayer book on his desk.'

Mr Thomas in spruce tussore, with his coat hanging behind his chair and the silver buckles on his new pair of braces gleaming, took the book with the neutral air of a judge handling a document tendered in evidence. He unfolded his gold-rimmed spectacles, breathed moisture on them and cleaned the lenses slowly. He did this with a rectangular piece of tissue paper of the sort placed under the gummed flaps of envelopes to prevent them sticking in the heat. He folded the tissue paper meticulously to a small bundle and dropped it in the waste paper basket. Then he put on his glasses and looked at the book.

Momoh hovered about, waiting for the verdict.

'This is Latin; this is what they call the classics. Amo, amavi, amatum, amare; first conjugation, 'to love', I love, I have loved, to have loved and lost, that sort of thing.' He looked through the pages with the hopeless air of a connoisseur examining an objet d'art which he had first rejected then

returned to buy and found it sold. 'I could have gone to college if I had wanted to, but I wanted to get on. I was young then', he added reminiscently. His manner changed 'Classics indeed, with those annual reports six weeks overdue. Some people have no idea of Her Majesty's time. Here, take it back', he said handing it to Momoh. Momoh took the book gingerly and tiptoed off with it, vastly impressed with Mr Thomas's display of learning and at the same time with his hard-headed down-to-earth efficiency.

As he placed it down again in the inner office, Sanderson walked in, in soft shoes. Momoh dropped it hurriedly with a start. 'Reading my love-letters?' Sanderson called cheerfully.

'Oh no, Sir, n—no Sir', he stammered. 'I was just looking for a file', and he grabbed at the nearest one and read out: "Marriage, Customs local—Laws and Regulations F.132". Yes, this one Sir.'

★   ★   ★

Father Horgan turned up to see Sanderson later in the morning. The annual inspection of his mission schools was drawing near. It was on this usually that the Government grants for the year depended. Father Horgan was a little man with nervous jerky movements which always seemed curiously to disappear completely when he sat down and folded his arms, but on standing he was always on the move, gesticulating slightly, removing his glasses, polishing them, replacing them, and dangling his sun helmet by its precarious worn leather strap. He passed by Mr Thomas's desk saying 'Good morning' very cheerfully, gave Momoh a friendly nod, and entered Sanderson's office.

'Aha! Aha!' he gave a little shout, his head jerking a little to one side, 'Still enveloped with work, I see.'

'Quite enveloped and very much behind hand', Sanderson replied. 'Do sit down', he added.

Father Horgan prowled about, twisting a handkerchief. He pounced upon the classical text which Momoh had carefully replaced on the desk.

'Are you proposing to rebuild the British Empire on the model of Rome?' he asked.

'Temporal or Spiritual?'

Father Horgan laughed delightedly, rubbing his hands, walking towards the window and back. Sanderson was a little surprised and gratified at his own sally of wit and its success.

'But seriously, Richard,' Father Horgan began in a different tone of voice—the padre speaking to a brother officer, the chaplain discussing a point with a third-year man—'What do you think about the benefits of teaching the ancient tongues to the African? One sometimes needs the advice of a lay, unprejudiced mind on these educational matters. After all, my boys are going to live in a world of men, not schoolmasters.'

'I think it is valuable myself,' he continued, answering his own question, 'as knowledge itself. And apart from that I can hardly see how they can be expected to learn and understand English without being aware of its origins. They ought to begin from the Latin', he said, giving a glance of marked approval at Sanderson's book. 'I'd have started it in my secondary school, only one is so hampered by lack of funds. It's so cramping, I wonder often if you people realise how much we help you.'

'We know, we know', Sanderson replied soothingly. By then he had got used to the urgent intense way mission agents besieged the government for grants. At first it had surprised him as he was more familiar with the conscientious but slightly offhanded way his uncle had held annual missionary bazaars in the church hall at home. He smiled, looked at the tanned leathery face of the old priest and wondered what was coming next.

'You've forgotten the annual inspection or perhaps postponed it', Father Horgan hastily added, being tactful. He was not quite sure what Sanderson was like as the secular arm.

'Oh yes, the annual inspection.'

'Your predecessor liked to test my senior boys with some mathematical exercises,' Father Horgan hinted, 'but of course you will doubtless have your own method. When can we expect you?' he added anxiously.

Sanderson guessed that school-desks had probably been scrubbed, walls painted and pupils primed. In fact he had passed by the school that week and had noticed boys mowing grass with scythes and moving in and out with pails of water on their heads.

'Would tomorrow be too soon?'

'No, no, tomorrow will be splendid.' He paused wondering whether the untruth was worth it. Yes it might be, and anyhow it was partly true in a sense. 'We are always ready in fact, always spotlessly and absolutely ready for inspection.'

The next day, wearing the air of pleasant gravity he remembered that retired generals or distinguished old boys wore when handing out prizes on school speech days, Sanderson set out on his annual inspection accompanied by Father Horgan. He even wondered humorously whether he would be asked to make a speech afterwards, and what he would say. Perhaps a few words in the time-honoured tradition about what a poor and indifferent pupil he had been at school himself; and look what he was now, he reminded himself smiling—an acting District Officer. Beware of overstudy, there is no telling where it will end you. Perhaps only as an Assistant District Officer.

'You like our lawn then', Father Horgan said noticing his smile.

'Oh yes', Sanderson looked up from his reverie. 'I wish my gardener would take some lessons from your boys on mowing.'

Father Horgan tripped by happily, and his head jerked once or twice to one side. Things had started well. Perhaps he might be able to squeeze an increase for an additional pupil-master's salary this year, which he'd never been able to get from McPherson.

The latter had always inspected the school on the same day every year for ten years, and had always asked the same questions and recommended the same grants, in spite of Father Horgan's urgent pleas and broadest hints. Mr McPherson would ask the Senior class why two times two were equal to two to the second power, and three times three was not equal to three to the third power. Father Horgan had taught a generation of boys the answer to that one. Though he did not know it, McPherson was known to the African schoolboys as two-squared McPherson. The answer, by now almost official, was that in the first case it was simply a mathematical coincidence. Words which McPherson himself had once told Father Horgan and forgotten.

This answer would always surprise and please McPherson. 'I would have used exactly the same words myself', he would say, turning round to the old Irish priest. 'Obviously there is nothing wrong with standards here. Your grant will certainly be recommended.' And with that he would march firmly back to his office. Sanderson had heard all about this from Momoh, who had attended the school. He decided to vary the question.

'And these are the Seniors', Father Horgan led the way into the small classroom.

'Class, attention!' the head boy said smartly.

'Good Morning Father Horgan, Good Morning Sir', the class chorused.

'Sit down, sit down, boys. Mr Sanderson, may I introduce Mr Kamara, one of our masters.'

Sanderson approached the young African master with outstretched hand.

'How do you do, Mr Kamara', he said, shaking hands warmly.

'I am quite well, Sir, thank you', Kamara replied, smiling nervously.

'Mr Sanderson the D.O. has come to visit us, boys', Father Horgan said, turning round to the class with forced cheerfulness, 'to see how you are getting on.' Sanderson turned too and distinctly heard Kamara mouthing softly behind his back

—'Math-e-mat-ic-al Co-in-cidence', for the benefit of the more forgetful of the boys.

'What is Empire Day?' Sanderson asked wickedly.

The air was charged with disaster. Father Horgan was breathing noisily. Sanderson pointed to a boy who had been half hidden—at the back of the class. 'In the first case it is simply a Mathematical Coincidence', the boy said with a matter-of-fact air, finishing almost before he had stood up properly.

Father Horgan took matters into his own hands.

'What is Empire Day, as taught in your Civics class?' he asked sternly.

Obviously the matter was a bit clearer now. A few arms shot up, in what at first seemed a Fascist salute, or some national-ist sign. He looked inquiringly at Father Horgan.

'Those boys are expressing willingness to answer your question.' Sanderson pointed to a smiling youngster near the front. The arms all went down and the boy stood up.

'Empire Day is a public holiday, Sir, when we have a march past the Governor and the Police Band plays.' He sat down again with the self-congratulatory air of one who had saved a hopeless situation.

'Yes but what does it celebrate?'

The arms shot up again. The boy who had just sat down looked round with dismay and then turned round again with the slight shrug of one who had done his best. Sanderson pointed to another.

'Empire Day celebrates a great and glorious victory of the Queen of England.'

'Over whom?' Sanderson asked, himself confused with memories of Blenheim.

'Over her enemies', the boy said with a surprised air, sitting down. Sanderson was at a loss but he tried another.

'Empire Day was the day the Great and Glorious Victoria, Queen of England was bonded.'

'Bonded?' Sanderson asked, 'You mean borr ...,' he paused inquiringly, trying to help. The boy stood, a bit confused, and then dim and scattered memories of the more hectic portions of English history coming back, his face cleared.

'Ah yes, thank you, Sir.' He started again halfway. '.... the day the great and glorious Victoria was burnt in the rain.'

'Burnt in the rain! But how is that possible?' Sanderson asked.

Father Horgan wrung his hands in despair. Mr Kamara hung his head with shame. Sanderson himself was a bit upset at the cataclysm he had caused. He searched around quickly with his eyes, and caught sight of a youngster who unlike the others had not raised his arm but was looking down with a veiled look of mystery and a slight smile of superior knowledge. He was sitting in the front row and Sanderson gently tapped him on the shoulder. From the audible sighs of relief behind him Sanderson knew he had chosen the best pupil in the class and that the situation was saved.

The boy cleared his throat and faithfully repeated his lesson.

'Empire Day was the day the great and glorious Victoria, Queen of England was born. Her reign was a long and successful one and during it the British Empire was extended and established. It falls on May 24th.'

'Thank you', said Sanderson. The sentence 'I would have used the same words myself', hovered on his lips. But no, that would be unkind, he thought. I've created enough havoc in one afternoon as it is.

He walked out with Father Horgan. 'Your grant is safe for this year, Father', he said, shaking hands as he left.

'You are too kind, Mr Sanderson, too kind', Father Horgan answered.

*   *   *

Sanderson sent his hammock away and with one of his court messengers, really a mixture of military policeman and office boy, set out in the direction of the market. He felt in an inspecting mood this morning and the sun was not yet too hot. He tried to converse in the African language with the court messenger. He always seized an opportunity to do this in preparation for the language test which each officer of the Administrative Service had to take before confirmation of his appointment. The tall powerfully built African walked slightly in front of him pushing aside the twigs of branches overhanging the path. He smiled respectfully when Sanderson addressed him and answered in English with as good an accent as he could, to show that he should be promoted a corporal and interpreter if the opportunity offered.

Sanderson gave up the struggle early and they trudged on silently. Sometimes a bird would be disturbed by the noise of a cracking twig and would veer off angrily, chirping, its plumage an iridescent streak of red, green and blue, to settle on a higher branch. They soon came to a clearing where there was a long low shed and some huge cotton trees. This was the market and it was crowded with people from neighbouring villages buying, selling, bartering and gossiping. The women sat with easy grace on low stools with their wares on mats spread on the ground in front of them under the shade of the trees. The more successful ones were in the shed with their goods on rickety stalls. There were only women and children about except at one or two of the larger stalls where grave middle-aged men sat aloof from the gossiping women.

The women had their hair done up in elaborate plaits half concealed under gay cotton scarves. They had on simple dyed cloth wrapped around their body from the knees to just above the breast and some wore blouses. The children played about in the dust while the older ones organised themselves into bands and raided stalls or played complicated games, chanting and clapping as they did so. The mats on the ground and the stalls in the shed were crowded with goods and foodstuffs of all descriptions. Dried fish, salted fish and raw fish; okras, sorrel leaves, and red pepper; cassava, sweet potatoes, bananas, and plantains; rice, and ground-nut and millet seed heaped up in separate piles in pyramid form with the apex crowned with the cylindrical cigarette tin as measure; palm-oil, ground-nut oil, and coconut oil placed in empty gin bottles and stoppered with a bit of rag or crumpled paper; little oil lamps and dishes made from kerosene tins; some scrawny fowls and guinea-hens lying on the ground with their feet tied, squawking and flapping their wings, all added to the general bustle of the whole scene.

There was a mild consternation when Sanderson and the court messenger arrived. The latter moved in front, kicking mats right and left and swishing his cane amidst a chorus of abuse from the women. He was trying to clear a path for Sanderson, who however restrained him. They then threaded their way forward, the court messenger with firm strides sometimes trampling on goods, whilst Sanderson skipped and leaped across mats. He stopped for a moment to look at an attractive brown toddler of about three bending over to build its own heap of rice. The child looked up and on seeing Sanderson screamed with fright and rushed to hide behind its mother, clutching her wrapper and hiding its face frantically.

'Look, you,' the mother scolded, 'do you want to drag off my cloth and leave me naked? Hush, hush,' she soothed the child in her language which she thought Sanderson would not understand, 'come out and watch him. The white man won't eat you. He is the same as you are only his skin is peeled and scalded white or else he could be your father. Come, come and look at him, he may want to take your photo and who knows may give you a penny with a hole in the middle.' The child slowly uncovered its face and shyly looked out, then stretched out its hand with its white upturned palm. Sanderson smiled and put a penny in it and walked on. About a dozen older children pursued him instantly crying out for pennies. The court messenger turned round suddenly and lunging forward, struck out at the nearest two or three and they scattered shrieking.

Sanderson entered the shed bravely although by now feeling slightly sick with the smell of smoked fish, cow-dung and dust. Looked around. The largest stall was groaning with meat and fish. It bore a faded painted sign to emphasize its importance. Sanderson deciphered it.

Mr A. J. Y. K. BAWA, ESQ.,
      Wholesale and Retail Merchant,
            Cash Terms only. No Credit.
Motto: Buy quickly. Today we live, Tomorrow we die.
            Bawa for ever.

He looked around for the immortal salesman.

'Yes, sah, what goods do I purchase you? Me ex-service-man.' Sanderson started slightly at the voice coming suddenly from behind and turned round to face an intelligent-looking man bustling past to stand behind the stall. He was short and stocky and wore a clean vest, a frayed blue black coat and a dyed blue wrapper round his waist and legs, instead of trousers. He had on a tropical military hat, broad brimmed with one side lifted up and buttoned to the crown. He gravely saluted and stood up at attention with his head cocked to one side.

'At ease', Sanderson said, entering into the spirit of the thing.

'Yes sah, me Bawa. Today we live', he added identifying himself further and relaxing. 'You ex-service too, I see,' he continued, wanting a little conversation. He felt his prestige increasing in the open view of the whole market. He turned slightly towards Sanderson, and away from the court messenger, excluding him, the arrogant fellow, he'd decided. The other, secure in his blue uniform edged with red, stood apart looking away into the distance strongly disapproving of it all and washing his hands of the whole matter.

'Yes, I'm ex-service too, Mr Bawa', Sanderson said savouring the atmosphere of the British Legion, the regimental dinner, the reunion of good fellows.

'I fight in East Africa,' Bawa continued, 'I fight in Burma and I fight in London.' He paused musing. 'Ah, but the fight in London was good. Only too much Irish potatoes and too much sausages.'

'Why did you fight in London?'

'Well, not so much a fight', Bawa explained. 'It was a parade, a victory parade. We camp in London near the big gravestone of King Albert, the big Queen's man.'

'Oh, I see, you were in Kensington Gardens.' Sanderson noted that the time was getting on and that the small crowd around the stall was growing. He decided to move on. 'You must come and tell me some more about this sometime. By the way,' he said, to satisfy his official conscience and partly to mollify the court messenger, 'what's the price of a bottle of your palm oil?' Bawa looked hurt at this intrusion of business into what he had skilfully transformed into an important social call. Anyway, he thought, you can never tell with white men. Then to his alarm he discovered that he had forgotten the control price, which most of the traders usually ignored. He was confused momentarily. Then with great presence of mind he threw out his arms expansively. He cried in an injured tone, 'I give it to you. How much bottle do you want? One? Two? Three?' He turned away, into the back of the stall, where he swiftly consulted the control price list which had been conveniently hidden under the shelves from the gaze of his few literate customers.

'Well, say I were not an ex-serviceman,' Sanderson pursued, 'what would you have charged me?'

'One and three pence, the control price, of course', Mbanya answered, trying to look hurt and triumphant at the same time —with some success.

*　　*　　*

The months wore on, and the rains dwindled, and the cool Harmattan wind began to blow steadily from the Sahara to the distant unseen Atlantic. It filled the tiny British population with renewed vigour and gave an extra spring to their step. The local Africans put on thick pullovers and heavy scarves, complained of the weather and kept indoors to avoid catching cold.

In the end Sanderson had to his shame struck out no new line in writing his report, but had simply fashioned something out in the old way. After all, he thought, he was only temporarily in charge and it was dangerous to create reckless precedents. Continuity was the thing, he reminded himself. Continuity was the thing for a deputy. Time enough for originality when he would be in charge somewhere. He went up to the club two or three evenings a week and noticed with amusement that as acting D.O. opinions were now and again deferred to his. He was asked once to give a lecture to the African Club which consisted largely of clerks, school teachers and the local agent of a political newspaper.

Sanderson's talk had been on Roman Britain. He had

chosen this because he felt it to be strictly non-controversial, and in fact the whole thing was a rehash of a talk he'd given on an Army education course. He soon however found himself in deep waters. First, when an old retired African schoolmaster had got up and fiercely argued the dates of the Roman landings, Sanderson agreed with him hastily, and the old man had sat down again muttering and glaring like a man who had nearly been cheated of the truth had he not been more vigilant. The journalist next stood up and asked with guile, 'Did Mr Sanderson say that Roman Britain was like Kissiland today?'

'Yes, in some ways', Sanderson answered guardedly.

'The speaker means that we are 2,000 years behind Britain, no doubt.'

'I do not', Sanderson replied.

'Anyway he means we are centuries behind Britain, I take it', the journalist said, sitting down.

'I meant nothing of the sort', Sanderson said rather sharply. The journalist stood up again.

'I must have misunderstood the speaker then', he said heavily. 'But whilst I am about it may I ask one or two things?' he said, turning to the African Chairman.

The latter was indecisive and started 'I am afraid we haven't time....'

The journalist ignored him and turned again to Sanderson, rapidly opening a folded piece of paper in his hand and harangued the meeting for five minutes on British Imperialism. Some members looked embarrassed. Some were secretly pleased, and some looked keenly at Sanderson to see how he was taking it. Sanderson with crossed legs and folded arms smiled and fastened his eyes determinedly on his notes lying on the table near him. He did not reply. After the journalist there was silence. Then the old schoolmaster got up again and asked whether any Roman remains had been discovered recently in Britain, and whether the British Government intended to return them to their rightful heirs and owners, the present Italian people. Sanderson ruffled his notes and smiled into them, trying to hide his face.

Such Roman remains as had been found, he explained, were mainly mosaic pavements, broken pottery and Roman roads, and ditches. 'It might well prove impracticable to return these', he added.

The meeting eventually ended peaceably. The young wife of a junior clerk moved a charming vote of thanks, speaking, Sanderson noticed, directly and seemingly impromptu.

'Some of us are more interested in the political side of things,' she said, 'but perhaps there are more lasting matters in this subject which interest the majority in this society.' The old schoolmaster seconded the vote of thanks in a short speech, now and again adjusting his spectacles to read Latin quotations which he had copied out in his pocket notebook. He came up afterwards and shook hands with Sanderson, congratulating him on his talk.

During his lecture Sanderson's eyes had roamed round the room at his audience, at the carbide acetylene lamp fizzing gently from its hook, illuminating the grave dark faces of the score or so of men and women sitting before him, a few of the older men taking notes, and one or two children sitting on their mothers' laps gently dozing. It seemed a bit unreal to him and yet he felt this must be some kind of reality. These people were townspeople from the coast who for one reason or another had found themselves away in the hinterland by the fastness of the Kissi mountains; with one or two educated Kissilanders invited, they had formed a literary club to keep the flags of culture flying, they earnestly thought; in the same way, Sanderson mused sardonically, as was done in the European club—drinking, playing bridge and thumbing through back numbers of *The Tatler and The Illustrated London News.* He saw Mr Thomas in the back row looking at him encouragingly. Mr Thomas had thawed when Sanderson had at last finished the annual report. Momoh and two other Kissilanders were sitting in the front row as guests of honour. Sanderson had an absurd desire to ask all of them round to his bungalow to drink beer and continue the discussion but he saw how improbable it would be, and he wilted before their serried ranks of quiet and impregnable respectability. They are all probably teetotallers, he decided. He left at the end of the meeting after promising to attend future ones if he could. He drove home, bumping gently on the uneven dusty road wondering, as he often did about educated Africans, in what way they'd discuss him afterwards, or if at all.

⋆ ⋆ ⋆

Momoh reminded Sanderson, one day, that the P.W.D. Headquarters Engineer would be coming from the capital in a week's time. Momoh had put into operation the simple pro-cedures required—the rest house to be got ready, the file for maintenance and repair of Government buildings to be gone through and new requirements determined or invented; the Government lorry to be got ready in case that of the visiting engineer broke down on the way to Kissi or when returning from it. Sanderson looked through the list, initialled his approval and asked Momoh the name of the engineer.

'Mr O. E. Jones, Sir', Momoh replied with a suppressed smile of pride which puzzled Sanderson at the time, as he remembered afterwards.

Sanderson couldn't place Jones, and the name did not sound familiar. Must be new, he thought, and decided to look him up in the most recent Blue Book. He ran his finger down the column of the Senior P.W.D. staff until he came to the J's. Ah, there it was, 'Jones, Olayemi, Egbert'. Oh, that was it, he was an African. That was why he hadn't heard of him before. He whistled softly to himself. By jove, there might be complications. Usually visiting members of the senior service were taken to the European Club on those evenings which they spent in Kissi. He began to go through the list of members in his mind one by one, trying to guess what their reactions would be to an African guest. Then he wondered for a moment a bit shamefacedly whether it wasn't he who had started making excuses and finding reasons before anything happened. But no, he decided, it was his duty to make sure, beforehand that there wasn't an incident, because if there was he would have to make a report and probably bear the unspoken blame from Headquarters. He wondered whether it would not be wiser to ask old Mr Thomas the senior African clerk to entertain Jones. At last he made a decision—he knew what he would do. He would ask Jones to dinner himself at his bungalow and he would ask Hounslow, the agent of a large firm, to make a third. Hounslow was English but born in East Africa, son of a Kenya settler. He would show by that that he had no prejudice. With that problem solved he turned to work with a lighter heart but with a vague sense of dissatisfaction.

*   *   *

Jones arrived promptly on the day he was scheduled to arrive, just after lunch. He was a tall, youngish man, probably in his early thirties with a small, army moustache, close cropped hair, very dark skin and even white teeth; he was completely un-smiling, and very polite. He shook hands with Sanderson, accepted a seat, refused a cigarette and got down to business almost immediately. He listened to Sanderson carefully, made notes and asked one or two questions. Sanderson called Momoh and asked him to bring in the files. The clerk brought these in, put them down and was going away, when Sanderson suddenly remembering his smile of pride, stopped him, and introduced him to Jones who smiled pleasantly and briefly, shook hands and then turned again to the files. Sanderson found this politeness and efficiency a bit uncomfortable at first and tried to soften the atmosphere with a joke here and there. But Jones either did not understand or pretended he did not understand. At the end of a couple of hours most of the work was finished. Sanderson asked Jones what he hoped to do that night, and then feeling that the African engineer might regard it as an unwarrantable intrusion into his privacy he hastily added, 'Because I'd like you to come to dinner with me.'

'Yes thank you, that will be nice', Jones answered, packing up his notes and getting up. Sanderson was a little disappointed that he hadn't shown much enthusiasm or pleasure. Hang it all, he thought, I don't suppose many Europeans would ask him as I have done; perhaps he is political, and he is only accepting out of a sense of duty. 'You are sure you can manage it, by the way', he said aloud.

'Oh yes, thank you, that would be very nice', Jones repeated. 'I'll go and see the other official buildings you men-tioned, but will be free this evening.' He is asking me because he hasn't the courage to take me to their club, Jones thought; these blighters, he probably wants a new refrigerator too. Ah well! 'Goodbye then, for the present', he said to Sanderson, who walked with him to the door and shook hands again whilst Momoh looked on admiringly.

Hounslow appeared at seven at Sanderson's bungalow and mixed himself a drink. He shouted through the door to Sanderson who was changing in his bedroom. 'Is anyone else coming tonight?'

'Jones, the new assistant engineer', Sanderson shouted back.

'What's he like? Does he come from Swansea, look you, man?'

'No, he is an African—Mr Olayemi Egbert Jones.'

There was a pause.

'Are you there, Hounslow?' Sanderson asked anxiously after a while.

'Yes, I am', Hounslow replied through the door. 'Why didn't you tell me this before?'

'Because frankly, I wasn't sure whether you'd come.'

'Are you afraid, Sanderson, of facing an educated black alone?'

'No, not at all, but I thought it would be good experience for you, my lad. It might correct some of your slave-driving ideas.'

'I am afraid he and I won't find much to say to each other', Hounslow replied. 'Pity the Club's closed tonight, or I would have escaped before he arrived.'

Sanderson opened the door and entered the lounge-cum-dining room.

'The Club's closed?'

'Yes', Hounslow said. 'A peculiar situation has arisen. We've run out of drinks, through bad management', he added. 'Why, were you going to take your Mr Jones there?'

'The idea had somehow occurred to me', Sanderson said, feeling relieved and a little ashamed.

'There's no end to what you wallahs in the administrative would do to show your official broad-mindedness. Is he political?' he asked.

'I shouldn't wonder', Sanderson answered. 'They all are, these chaps, you know, although they've got to conceal it when they are in the service.'

'Shouldn't be surprised if he supplies copy to nationalist newspapers. However we must move with the times', Hounslow said resignedly. 'He'll probably get drunk and start smashing bottles', he added hopefully.

*   *   *

Ola Jones soon appeared looking very smart in light grey tropical suiting and a college tie.

Hounslow and Jones were introduced to each other. The African said how do you do. The Kenya white nodded. Neither shook hands. Sanderson mixed drinks and made

conversation about his garden. They moved over to the other side of the room and sat down to dinner. Sanderson waited for Jones to begin before he started. Jones waited for Sanderson to begin because the latter was more senior in the service and in any case the array of knives and forks was a little confusing and he was not too sure which to begin with. Hounslow started as soon as the hors d'œuvre was placed in front of him. Then Sanderson put his knife and fork on his plate and passed Jones the salt. Jones took this and then started. Hounslow concentrated on the food and ate gloomily and slowly, now and again addressing a remark to Sanderson. Jones, perhaps noticing this, turned slightly to Sanderson and spoke to him exclusively of his afternoon's work. Towards the end of the meal Hounslow, talking about rising prices, turned to Jones and said,

'How are your people managing, Mr Jones, with all these rising prices; I suppose they are finding European food and clothes not quite so easy to maintain as they thought, eh?'

Jones chewed his food in silence for a few minutes. The silence was becoming unbearable. Hounslow was beginning to frown, thinking he had been snubbed, and was going to repeat his question in a louder voice. Sanderson thought the African was annoyed and was going to say something tactful. Jones sipped some water, swallowed it and then turning to Hounslow said,

'Yes, they are finding European food and clothes hard to maintain.' Then he continued eating.

Hounslow wasn't sure whether sarcasm was meant, and he searched the African's face unsuccessfully for some sign. Sanderson said something about the rise in the cost of living hitting all classes, high and low, except the very rich, of course, 'among which I daresay none of us are numbered', he ended.

He stood up. 'Let's go out and sit in more comfortable chairs and have our coffee.'

Hounslow decided to relax as he did not want to be boorish. He felt curious to know what Africans really thought, as he had never had the opportunity of talking to an African in an atmosphere of equality. He addressed questions now and again to Jones about what Africans thought on this or that matter, until the latter replied quietly that he was afraid he'd been so busy lately he'd lost touch a bit with the opinion of his people. Hounslow glanced sharply again to see whether any offence had been meant. Trouble is, he said to himself, you can never tell whether these educated natives mean to be insolent or not. They all wear this damned mask of politeness, haven't the courage of their convictions. As the evening wore on and another bottle of whisky was opened, the atmosphere became more convivial. Sanderson turned to Jones suddenly and said, 'Look here, Ola, do you chaps hate us? I mean us, the English?'

Although feeling warm with the good fellowship and whisky a trace of guardedness crept over Jones' face. Sanderson noticed it and said, 'Oh, of course this is all off the record. We are speaking as man to man. I mean to say, I would regard you as a member of my class, both here and in England. But in general are we hated?'

'I don't think so', said Jones, 'at least, not continuously.'

'You would admit that we are hated, then', Hounslow said, coming in, 'sometimes anyhow?' He leant back feeling he had scored.

'Don't you hate us too sometimes?' Jones countered smiling.

'The psychologists say it's a good thing to hate well and to love well. After all, it's the hatred of the things evil which make the great social reformers, but to return to the point, do you dislike us?'

'Well, you are sometimes very proud you know', Jones answered. 'One might not dislike you, but whoever he is, white or black, everybody likes to see a proud man humbled occasionally. I don't mind you personally', he said hurriedly, 'Good heavens, on, nor you either, Mr Hounslow.'

'Call me Hounslow, old fellow. But tell me seriously, do you think you chaps can run this country without our help? The white man has a stake in this country, and he's done as much for it in a generation as you haven't done for centuries.'

'How do you know it's the white man and not the age we live in which has done the miracle? How do you know that we couldn't have done it ourselves, given the opportunity in this age?'

'Ah, I thought you would say that.' Hounslow leaned forward, 'but how then do you explain the presence in the middle of this century of naked tribesmen on the Jos Plateau and of the naked Masai in East Africa drinking the blood of their cattle; that is, all the savagery in places in Africa where the white man has not spread his influence?'

Jones replied mildly and without heat, 'There are more Europeans in Jos than in any other place in Nigeria, and there are more Europeans in Kenya than there are in any other country in East Africa. I suppose those are well established statistical facts, are they not?' he said, turning to Sanderson.

'I believe so,' the latter replied; he continued after a pause, 'although to counterbalance the backwardness of the Plateau people and the Masai a great many advances have otherwise been made there and elsewhere.'

'Oh, quite so,' said Jones, 'quite so.'

The conversation halted for a while in polite silence. An air of reasonableness hung in the atmosphere.

Hounslow felt obscurely worsted by the African but rescued by Sanderson. He did not like the situation too well but he contented himself with a noisy sip to express insouciance.

Sanderson turned to Jones suddenly and said, 'You trained at home didn't you? I mean in Britain? Where were you? London?'

'Yes, I was in London for most of the time, at one of the big Polytechnics near Oxford Circus. I lived in digs at Cricklewood and came up to the college every morning by bus.'

'Did you have good digs?' Sanderson asked.

Old Varsity men swapping reminiscences, Hounslow thought, a little contemptuously, stretching himself out on the chair easily. He will soon ask him, 'What was your first fifteen like', and the darkie will say, 'Actually the forwards were not bad, a bit slow at passing perhaps, but not bad at all; we once drew with Rosslyn Park....' He helped himself sternly to some more whisky.

'I found a room eventually,' Jones answered, 'after having several doors slammed in my face. It was quite a comfortable room and the landlady was a blonde, decent soul.'

Sanderson smiled. 'What a turn of phrase you have', he said. 'But seriously, apart from the lodgings problem, did you enjoy your time in England? Did you get to know us well?' Sanderson asked. 'Did you for instance stay with an English family?'

'I had an invitation once, from some church people, and I nearly went, but in the end I decided not to, because I am not particularly religious, and besides, my friends told me that English families would be patronising to me and would call the neighbours to come and see me at close quarters, like a strange beast.'

'Oh but come, come Jones, surely that's nonsense, you didn't believe that, did you? We used to have an Indian friend to come and stay regularly and we usually asked our friends to meet him, simply because it was the custom. And besides we were afraid he would be bored with just our company. You must realise an Englishman's home is his castle, you know, and when he lets down the drawbridge for you to come, you may be sure he likes you, and not for all the world would he do it otherwise, much less ask you a second time. You really didn't believe what your friends told you did you?'

'Well I didn't at first,' admitted Jones, 'but later on I wasn't so sure. It's the uncertainty of one's reception in England which confuses a lot of us. Sometimes you are welcomed with open arms by nice people. I can remember at least a very nice man I knew, called Cohen. But on the other hand you get sudden rebuffs. Or what is worse, people simply avoid you everywhere as if you had the plague or some infectious disease. They are just cold and distant.'

Sanderson filled up his glass slowly. 'I know what you mean', he said, sipping from his glass and then holding it up to the light with cupped hand and revolving it. 'I worked in London too for a few months, and I found people very cold and distant. I often wondered then whether there was something wrong with me. People behave very strangely in cities, you know, Jones. They tend to be secretive and shy as a protection against the vastness surrounding them, and anything stranger than usual, like a man with a dark complexion, makes it even more so.'

Hounslow chuckled. 'By jove you are quite the Oxford man, Sanderson', he said. 'You'll theorise your way to heaven and find it hellish when you get there.' He laughed at his own words, and then his brow swiftly darkened with heavy anger. 'You've got nothing to complain about', he said to Jones. 'Nor you either', turning to Sanderson. 'I was the disappointed one in England. I grew up in Kenya and we thought of England as home all the time, and our old man told us all sorts of stories of the English countryside and our heritage. But when I went there to school nobody seemed to bother about the things we held dear.' He stretched back again on the chair. 'I don't suppose it was a good school,' he continued, 'but it was a public school all right. Headmasters' Conference and all that. It was widely advertised in all the colonies, and they offered special cheap rates for holidays for boys whose parents were overseas. My father was a self-made man and left school early and when he heard about this school he thought he would make up to us educationally for what he himself had missed.'

'Did you go back to East Africa when you left school?' Sanderson asked.

'No, I stayed on for a bit longer. But things were never quite the same. I worked for a bit with a big exporting firm but didn't like it particularly. Some of the chaps there thought I was a bit of a blimp. They thought I was too narrow. People seemed to have changed so since my father's generation, whose ideas were what we colonials had. I mean white colonials of course', he added hastily

'And how did you find it changed from what you expected?' Jones asked conversationally.

'Oh, in all sorts of ways', Hounslow answered, after a short pause, during which he had debated whether to admit Jones freely into the conversation, and had decided that for free and easy social purposes the African could be an honorary white man for an evening. 'In all sorts of ways', he repeated reflectively nodding his head. 'Do you know', he said, tapping Sanderson's knee, 'that one evening a chap tried to elbow me out of the way at the end of a show, during the National Anthem? I was standing at the end of a row, and the fellow gave me lip. Said I was to move on as he had a bus to catch, and not to block the gangway. Of course I refused to move and stood at attention. The chap leaned over and said into my ear, 'Company at ease' in a terribly common accent. I stood unflinching and he and his gang climbed over the seats and clattered up. Must have been Communists of course. At the end of the 'Queen' I rushed down the foyer looking for him to knock him down. But by then they had gone. Things like that make me sad', he said, leaning back. 'No, the old country is not the same. Too much talk of freedom, equality and democracy, and not enough doing things.'

'I don't think they are as bad as that', put in Sanderson, feeling things were rather up to him. 'You'll find things changed in the larger cities, but curiously enough, London itself and the countryside remain always unchanged. What did you really think of London?' he said turning to Jones.

'Ah, London was full of wonders for me. It was the organisation of everything and the clockwork efficiency which amazed me. You English are efficient; I used to go for walks at night and watch the traffic lights changing from green to yellow to red to yellow to green again all through the night. When I was studying hard for exams I would go out at two to three in the morning to clear my brain before going to bed. Do you know I once saw a huge motor lorry actually stop at a cross-roads early one morning when the lights were against it. There was no one about, not even a policeman in sight and I was in the shadow. But he stopped just because the lights were against him. That's what I call organisation and a sense of the right thing. I never

shall forget that moment. Gentlemen, that moment sum-
marized London and the British for me.'

There was a pause for a few moments, and the other two
looked obviously impressed. Jones shut his eyes slightly and
thought again of the Cricklewood he had loved often, but had
hated sometimes with a weary home-sickness in the grey
winter.

'To London', he said suddenly, raising his glass.

'To London', the others murmured, 'God bless her!'

'But mind you I was glad to be back home', Jones added,
after a while, fearing they might think him a black Englishman,
which he most dreaded. 'There are things a man can do in
this country which a man cannot do in England.'

'For example?' Hounslow asked with some interest.

'Well you can start things single-handed, and finish them
before your own eyes here, whilst you'd have to be a genius to
do that in England.'

'I don't know about beginning and finishing things here,'
Sanderson began.

'I've built a bridge here,' Jones interrupted, 'I came by this
district last year, about four miles away from here, on the
Yolahun road and there was a dry stream bed which people
used as a short cut to the big market in the dry season, but in
the rainy season the stream is too swift for them to ford it and
it used to take them about two hours to make a detour to
cross it further up on the swinging rope bridge. In fact
that's why for generations you'd have a small famine in this
district during the rains, because most people simply did not
bother or could not travel properly to the large town to sell
their crops and buy food. I couldn't understand why someone
could not have thought of the simple idea of building a
bridge there.'

'Perhaps they thought of it during the rains, but forgot it in the dry season. That often happens in this country. Or again people may simply have accepted it.'

'So you built that bridge! I wondered about it', Sanderson said. 'I thought it was the army, but it looked too permanent for them.'

'I expect it's improved things quite a lot now, hasn't it?' Jones asked with great triumph.

Sanderson wondered whether it was kinder to leave the truth unsaid, because in fact the bridge was only seldom used by the villagers and only by motor transport. Someone had been drowned years ago at that point and the local legend had it that there was a water spirit there during the rains.

'Yes, I think it has improved things', he said aloud.

'That's much sooner than I expected', said Jones. 'Do you know some years ago someone was drowned there and people think there is a devil around there during the rains? In fact, I had to hire a more powerful medicine man to sacrifice a chicken on the site and pour some rum on the ground before the labourers would begin.'

'As you know, we prefer champagne. Break a bottle of the stuff over the prow of a ship as she slides off her hawsers for the first time to appease the old gods. Same as you, old man, same as you', Hounslow said with a jovial bucolic politeness to Jones.

'Of course I had the chicken and the rest of the rum for dinner that evening', Jones lied, trying to show that he'd treated the whole thing as a piece of whimsy to humour his workmen, and had never in the slightest intended taking it seriously. At the same time he thought Hounslow had been patronisingly polite and kind, trying to compare it with an English custom. He had seen a new ship being launched himself at a shipyard and had been awed by it. Of course the thing bore no comparison with the blood of a white chicken and the rum poured out by a simple misguided African. In fact during the launching in the Clydeside there had been a milord about. He'd been pointed out to him. The thing bore no comparison. Anyhow, he thought, perhaps I am too sensitive.

'I envy you chaps, engineers, doctors, agriculturists, and so on', Sanderson said, 'you begin things, you finish them and you see the result, but we never do. We never even know if we've begun. Nor when we finish. We never even know whether we are redundant.'

Jones was touched. 'Oh no, no,' he cried, 'you administrators, white or black, will always be needed to plan things and to manage men. When we are finished, as engineers, then we begin to learn your job, to administer. But I must go', he said springing up, 'I've got to set off early tomorrow. And I know you will forgive me.'

He shook hands with both, and swiftly disappeared, in spite of Sanderson's protesting that he could put him up for the night. And Hounslow pressing the other man's whisky on him to take just one more for the road.

*　　*　　*

After the African had left, Hounslow strolled up and down the room, stumbling a little. Then he stopped suddenly in front of Sanderson who was slowly puffing a pipe.

'Do you know, old man', he said in a voice of such tiredness that the other glanced up swiftly. 'Do you know that apropos of what you said a few minutes ago, I am beginning to feel particularly redundant in this damned country!' He sat down and rested his head on the edge of the table with his body sprawling loosely in the chair.

'But you are not an administrator,' Sanderson said, 'You are the senior agent of a very wealthy firm.'

'No, I'm feeling *de trop* in a different sort of way, especially when I meet educated natives like our mutual friend here this evening. They brought us up telling us as children that Africa was a white man's country, and that for centuries to come we were to help and teach the black man slowly and certainly what it had taken us hundreds of years to learn. But here in my own lifetime I see these people trained to do all sorts of things, and the trouble is, they sometimes do them well. Mind you, I don't say they are as good as we are. They can never be that.'

'Yes,' said Sanderson 'just as we couldn't be them if we tried. We and they are both different but good in our separate ways.'

'Yes, yes, I suppose you've got to say that in your position', Hounslow replied. 'But whatever you say, I don't think they can do it in a generation, old man, they'll crack up when things go badly. That chap Jones, for example, was frightened of the water ju-ju. I could see it in his face.' He poured himself some more whisky and swallowed it quickly. 'All the same, old man, they made us feel useless, old man, darned useless. You Whitehall chaps can't see that you are trying to push us, your own kith and kin, out into the cold. You'd be surprised how hard I found it to get this job. And now Headquarters are talking about training African assistant managers. As if I didn't know what that meant. Why are you always trying to be fair, you Johnnies? Always pushing us out into the cold?' He burst into tears. Sanderson came up and stood by him then sat on the edge of the table.

'Don't you think the country is big enough, for Jones and you and me? Jones has got to be here because it's his country.

You are here because no man can do everything in his own country. I think this idea of a man's country belonging to him is a phase we all pass through. We passed through it fifty years ago. Only his countryside and the profitless patches in his country belong to any man. The fat of the land is to the man who can get it, and when he gets it he then tries to belong to the country even more than those whose heritage it was. It is by this eternal recruitment of the fittest alien that great nations and privileged classes survive. And that is why you will always be here if you are good enough, Hounslow, and for no other reason.'

The other man had been listening with attention. 'I wish I'd been educated your way, Sanderson. I wish I knew what words meant, but I gather it's the survival of the fittest.'

'So you think there will be room for all of us ?' he said getting up and stretching. 'It's not a bad country, all said and done. A man can see results in it sometimes.'

'To Africa', Sanderson toasted gravely.

'Yes, yes, to Africa, white man's and black man's too', Hounslow nodding sipping. 'A last one before I go, one for the road, so to speak', he added, nodding all the time as if comforted but only half convinced. Sanderson picked up the bottle. But by then it was empty.

'Never mind', Hounslow said thickly, 'we'll have it in a soda.' He was feeling tired, sad and then happy.

Sanderson filled the glasses. The little pearly bubbles clung to the sides of the glasses and burst later on the surface. They tickled Hounslow's nostrils.

'Whom shall it be to this time ?' Sanderson asked.

'To you, to you, old man', Hounslow said affectionately. 'To you, old man, and me', he chuckled.

'And Ola Jones too ?' Sanderson added.

73

'Yes, him too', Hounslow agreed.

'In fact to all good chaps everywhere.'

Sanderson saw Hounslow off from the small courtyard in front of his bungalow. 'Are you sure you will be able to drive yourself home', he asked him.

'Positive old man, I can drive home blindfolded. Give us a shove, there's a good fellow.'

Sanderson heaved and pushed for a while before the car broke into life and careered off. It headed away in the opposite direction from the town and Sanderson shouted to Hounslow to stop and turn round. But the car was soon lost to sight, although the sound could be heard in the distance. Sanderson went indoors with misgiving and wearily prepared for bed.

Hounslow put the car into gear and roared up a hill. The throb of the engine filled him with exultant power as did an occasional gust of wind. He knew where he was going and he felt his head strangely clear. After about fifteen minutes, he slowed down and stopped. He bent over his wheel and listened to the shrill call of the cicadas and the deep bass croaking of the frogs.

These would stop suddenly sometimes and an eerie silence would then fill the heavy air. He put the headlamps on and then walked forward slowly in the broad beam of light to examine the bridge more closely. It was an ordinary one, but strong, concrete and with a simple hard grace. He stood in the middle of it and jumped up and down as one trying a spring mattress, half-hoping it would break. He leaned over one side and watched the growing waters swirling between the rocks. He threw a twig in on one side and rushed over to the other side to see it appear. He laughed with pleasure when it did. Then he walked back slowly to his car. And Ola

Jones, standing in the shadows, where he had hidden when he had first heard the car, marvelled that Hounslow had not detected his presence, because his heart had been beating so. He had walked far out of town to come and see the bridge he had fashioned with love and care. He had come in the dark night, defying the dark to show himself that he was not afriad of the water-spirits. He had been strangely pleased although little puzzled at the look on the white man's face as the latter strode past slowly.

It leaped suddenly into the middle of the road and stood there poised, dazzled by the light from the headlamps. Hounslow sat upright in the driver's seat to watch it. Jones restrained a startled cry and gazed with fascination. It was a curious beast. It had the shape of an antelope but was reddish brown on its back and white underneath with a boundary line between the two colours as if it had been swimming and had washed off its colour underneath. It had slender curved horns on a head held proudly and supported on a delicate neck. It had black vertical stripes down each buttock and one on its back, continuing to the tail. It stood there for a few long seconds. Hounslow then sounded his horn sharply and the beast bounded high into the air and forward, to be lost as suddenly as it had appeared, like a secret memory.

'Oh, it's only a red-buck'; Hounslow voiced his thought. He started the car, reversed carefully into the side of the road and turned round and drove back steadily to town.

It was, after all, only a red-buck, an impala, that they were afraid of, Jones meditated as he climbed onto the bridge. He put the small spirit-level he always carried about with him on one of the railings and shone his torch on it. He nodded with satisfaction as he watched the air-bubble oscillate and settle in the centre; and then reluctantly, he started to walk back to the rest-house. He stopped suddenly, held out his hand a moment or so, and then broke into a steady run. For the rain had begun to fall in single heavy drops like the slow, quiet weeping of a woman proud, proud to distraction for an only son, yet vaguely afraid.